LUX ROSE 2

BORN TO KILL

CYN ALEXANDER

For Dream… Forever my baby.

CONTENTS

ACKNOWLEDGMENTS

Thank you so much to my readers! I hope you are enjoying this mini series before Anything for the Family Part 3 comes!
Don't worry! That will be out soon. I promise reading this mini series will help you really appreciate Lux in the rest of the Anything for the Family series.
I love you all - keep shining!

"Are you sure you have to go, papi?" Blanca asked with a pout on her sharp features. She was wrapped up in the white sheets the hotel provided while she perched sexily at the head of the bed, surrounded by pillows.

Mateo blew out a breath of air as he finished tying his shoelaces. His patience was thin as he turned to face Blanca. "Do you want this wedding to happen or not?"

Blanca sat up straighter with her brows knitted together. "Of course, I do. Probably more than Lux's clueless ass does."

Mateo stood. "Then I have to go. We've been holed up in this room for three days, and Lux has been asking when I'm coming home. I can't keep putting her off."

It was partly the truth. Lux had been asking him when he was going to come home, but it was only because she had a few jobs to take care of, and if he wasn't going to be there, then she was going to take them instead of her father. She didn't want to sit around bored while Mateo was working. If he was working, then so was she, but she had gotten back into town a few hours ago, and her questioning started back up again as soon as she got settled.

Mateo felt like he was being pulled in several directions, rightfully so. The women in his life, along with his poor decision making, were sure to be the death of him.

Blanca crawled over to him and perched on her knees, wrapping her arms around his neck while the sheet fell and exposed her naked body. Mateo instantly palmed her ass. She wasn't as thick as Lux, but she was damn sure holding her own. Slim thick was what he liked to call it, and her ass fit perfectly in his large hands.

"I guess you can go back to our bestie," Blanca replied wickedly. "Only a couple more weeks until you're married, eh? Not too much longer of sneaking around."

Blanca beamed, and Mateo nodded. "Right."

He was apprehensive as hell about how the next

month of his life would look. He had already lost so much when his parents died. He wasn't sure he was ready to lose Lux as well.

Blanca could tell he was getting inside his head, so she used her hand to direct his face so he was looking at her. When she was sure she had his full attention, she said, "You aren't having second thoughts, are you?"

Mateo had never hidden him not hating Lux. In fact, Blanca understood he loved Lux in his own way. He always had since they were children, and he spoke on that shit often. It hurt Blanca because she was in love with Mateo, but more than that, she was in love with the life she dreamed up once she killed her so-called best friend. It didn't matter how much Mateo confessed his love for Lux, Blanca was always right there to mind-fuck him and get him back on track with her plans. So, when Mateo looked at her with guilt-filled eyes, she knew what time it was.

"I just don't think we need to—"

Blanca cut him off with a kiss. Mateo was a weak ass man, because that kiss caused him to lose his train of thought. Just like that, Blanca had his mind gone. It was that easy for her. She literally had Mateo stuck on stupid, and she knew exactly which buttons to push in order to get what she wanted. When she finally pulled away, she gazed up at him with her dark eyes and said, "Papi, I love you. I know you have a thing with Lux, but you can't forget about everything we have worked so hard for. You're the only person I have aside from Aunt Dalia. I need you, Mat."

She forced tears to flood her eyes, and Mateo's eyes softened. On the inside, Blanca was smiling because she could see his resolve weakening. Mateo cleared his throat while his thoughts raced. He had a soft spot for Blanca. He felt bad for the way she grew up. Not that she had a terrible childhood or anything, just that her parents abandoned her and that she grew up poor. What Mateo didn't realize was that Blanca always had everything she ever needed. Dalia made sure of that, and Lux always took care of her in ways nobody else would ever understand because Lux didn't boast about the kind things she did, and Blanca wasn't about to hype Lux up to be this amazing person. The issue was that Blanca was greedy, and in her eyes, her life was terrible because it couldn't compare to Lux's.

Mateo leaned down and kissed her softly on the lips before saying, "I know, B. I got you. I just need to get my head right."

She smiled up at him. "You do. Now, go ahead and get back to Lux. I'll text you later, okay?"

He nodded. "Okay."

"Papi," Blanca said, catching his eye again. "It'll all be over soon, okay? No more sneaking around or living double lives. We will be able to rest easy soon enough. Just hang on for me a little bit longer, okay?"

He gave her a half smile and said, "Yeah, B. I hear you."

He turned to walk out of the hotel room they had been occupying. Just before he opened the door, Blanca said, "Don't forget to wash my pussy juices off your face before you speak to Lux."

She giggled as he shook his head with a smile and opened the door. Once it was closed behind him, she fell back onto the bed with a wide smile stretched across her face. She knew the next couple of weeks would be hard to keep Mateo on track, but she had just the remedy for that because not a damn thing was going to stop her from getting everything she wanted. Her pussy and mind games would keep him in check, and she knew she would have to work overtime in both ways to get him down the aisle and a bullet in Lux's head.

She rolled over and called the front desk of the hotel first, which happened to be her job. After speaking with the manager, she hung up, glad she was able to reduce her hours for the next month. She wanted to quit the bullshit ass job altogether since she would be filthy rich soon, but she knew she had to keep up appearances. She had one more phone call to make, so she scrolled through her phone and found her bestie's name before clicking the contact with an evil grin on her face.

Mateo did as he was told. The first thing he did when he got to the Rose household was go to the second floor where his room was, and he took a shower, cleansing himself of any trace of Blanca. Lux didn't know it, but he used that room more than she knew. Namely, the bathroom. He went in there after every link up with Blanca and made sure his shit was together before he made himself known to Lux.

When he was finished and dressed in fresh clothes, he made his way up to the third floor and found Lux hanging out in her TV room. She was curled up on a loveseat with a blue fuzzy blanket, and her hair was piled on the top of her head in a messy bun. He leaned on the doorframe and took her in. He loved seeing her like that. Natural and candid.

Without turning around, she said, "You gonna just stare, papi? Or are you going to come show me some love?"

Mateo chuckled. Since they were kids, he tried sneaking up on Lux, and it never worked. She had a strange sixth sense about shit like that, and after a while, he gave up.

He moved into the room and sat on the loveseat next to her, pulling her legs into his lap. "Hey, mami."

He leaned over and placed a kiss on her forehead, and when he did that, his heart pained a little. He knew there wouldn't be many more times he could do that to her, and it made him sad. It made him want to love on her more while also pulling away from her more. He was so conflicted. One thing he knew for certain, he didn't want Lux dead. No matter how hard he tried convincing Blanca that there was another way, she refused to let go of her vision of things. At the end of the day, Mateo knew Lux didn't deserve to die, but he also felt like Blanca deserved a good life. She grew to hate Lux as they got older, and in her mind, this was the only way to handle things. He somehow managed to get trapped right in the middle, but he felt he was too far in to go back now.

Lux picked up on his somber mood right away, and she immediately connected it to his parents' deaths. She fully believed he hadn't taken the proper time to grieve, and she hoped he was finished with work shit for a while so he could do that and help her prepare for their wedding. "You good, Mateo?"

He forced a smile. "Just tired. What are you watching?"

Lux eyed him for a moment. She knew him too well to know he wasn't just tired, but she decided to let it go, figuring he would open up to her when he was ready.

"*Criminal Minds*," she replied.

Mateo shook his head. "You have a weird obsession with serial killers, chaparrita. You know that?"

"You have no idea," Lux mumbled.

"What was that?"

"Nothing," she replied. "How was your business trip?"

Mateo shifted uncomfortably, but Lux didn't notice, because half her attention was back on the TV.

"It was fine," he replied vaguely. "How was yours?"

"It was fine," she copied his answer. Mateo wanted to ask more, but Lux beat him to the punch. "No more work until after the wedding, right?"

"Right," Mateo replied. He and Blanca had plans to link up at least once more before the wedding, but that was something he would have to deal with when the time came. He already warned Blanca he couldn't be missing for days on end again, and she said she understood. "I'm all yours until the wedding."

Lux beamed at him, showcasing her perfect teeth and a brilliant smile. She moved closer to him and nuzzled her nose into his neck before saying, "I hope you'll be all mine on the honeymoon and forever after, too."

Mateo laughed uncomfortably, because he didn't know what else to do. Of course, he wanted to promise her that, but how could he? If Blanca had it her way, Lux would be dead during their honeymoon and already spending her money. So instead of responding verbally, he kissed her forehead again, savoring the smell of her perfume, before he asked, "You got any plans for the night?"

She gestured toward the TV and replied, "This was pretty much it. I was thinking about ordering some food, but that's about it unless you have another suggestion."

Mateo shook his head and leaned back, making himself comfortable. "Nah, this seems perfect."

Lux nodded before she snuggled up to Mateo and focused on the show again. After a few moments, she said, "Oh, and B called. She wants to do lunch tomorrow, the three of us. I told her you were in."

Mateo played it cool, but on the inside, he instantly became nervous as hell. Any time he had them both in the same setting, his nerves were on ten. Plus, Blanca didn't mention anything about a lunch when he just saw her less than an hour ago, so he was left the rest of the night to ponder what the fuck she was up to.

ux woke up in a great mood. Her fiancé was finally home, and they were about to be married. Her nervousness subsided since he'd come home the night before, and she was thankful. She had two jobs while he was away, which made for four niggas she put six feet under in the last week. A bitch was tired and more than ready to hand the reins over to her father so she could focus on getting married to the love of her life.

Mateo, on the other hand, was not looking forward to the day, so he woke up in a terrible mood. Lux nudged him with her shoulder as they walked into their favorite Cuban restaurant called Victors. "Why the long face, papi? You been in a bad mood all morning."

Mateo straightened up and did his best to smile down at Lux, but she only furrowed her brows, so he sighed and said, "It's just work stuff, amor. Nothing to worry about."

He kissed the top of her head, and before Lux could pry any further, Blanca appeared behind them, having just arrived at the restaurant herself.

"Aw, aren't you two cute?" she said as she looked between the two.

Mateo immediately dropped his arm that had been around Lux's shoulders and grabbed at the back of his neck nervously.

"Hey, B!" Lux beamed at her best friend before hugging her tightly.

Blanca hugged her back, making sure to put on a show for Lux. Meanwhile, she blew a kiss at Mateo over Lux's shoulder. Mateo shook his head and immediately knew this outing was a bad idea. Blanca had been getting bolder lately, and the last thing he needed was Lux getting suspicious. He tried calling Blanca last night after Lux fell asleep, but she refused to answer her phone.

What Mateo didn't know was that she had dropped her hours at work, so she was only working a few shifts up until the wedding so she could keep an eye on his ass. She needed to make sure he followed through with their plan, so she planned on being all up in his grill from now until the wedding. If Lux was adamant about him being around over the next couple of weeks, then that meant Blanca's ass would be there, too. She was going to be suggesting all kinds of outings and plotting time for her and Mateo to sneak away privately from time to time, too, so she could throw her pussy at him and remind him of whose team he was really on.

When the two friends pulled apart, Blanca beamed up at Mateo as if she hadn't just seen him the previous day and held her arms out to him. "Qué pasa, Mat?"

"De nada," Mateo replied dryly as he gave Blanca a one-armed hug.

Lux sucked her teeth and looped her arm through Blanca's. "Don't mind him, chica. He's been in a foul mood all morning."

"Is that right?" Blanca asked as she looked over at Mateo with an arched brow.

Before Mateo could respond, a hostess appeared at the front stand and asked, "How many?"

"Just us three," Lux replied happily.

The hostess counted out three menus and gestured for the trio to follow her. When they made it to their booth, Blanca slid in next to Lux before Mateo could, leaving him to sit opposite them. His nerves were shot, but he calmed a little when he realized Blanca wanted this wedding to happen more than anyone. She wasn't about to do anything to fuck up her bag and her future with him. Still, that didn't mean she didn't intend to fuck with Mateo a little bit. She honestly loved to see his ass sweat. It was entertaining to her. More than that, though, she loved knowing she was making Lux out to be the biggest fool known to man. When she found out what Mateo and Blanca had been doing behind their backs... ahh... Blanca lived for that day. Truly.

"A little over two weeks. How are you two feeling?" Blanca asked after they got situated and were handed their menus. She looked over the menu nonchalantly while she waited for one of them to respond. Mateo's jaw clenched, but he didn't say anything, which was fine because Lux was happy to reply to her best friend.

"It's unbelievable, isn't it? We've been talking about it for so long... and it's finally about to be here. I'm getting excited, B. Like, for real," Lux gushed.

Blanca placed a smile on her face and said, "I'm excited too. We definitely have been waiting a long time."

She made eye contact with Mateo while she spoke, and he subtly shook his head, fully understanding the true meaning behind her words.

"Oh, papi, wait until you see our bestie in her bridesmaid's dress. She is so fucking *bad*," Lux said happily, glancing over at Mateo.

Mateo stiffened slightly, but he recovered before replying, "I'm more so ready to see you in your dress, mami."

Blanca cut her eyes at him and said, "Damn, that's how you do me? Can't let me shine for one second, huh?"

Lux giggled, thinking it was a joke. Mateo and Blanca were known to banter like this when the three of them were together, and she always got a kick out of it. The three of them had known each other for so long, they knew exactly how to press each other's buttons.

Lux stepped in and interrupted their banter. "Don't worry, B. You'll be the center of attention while you walk down the aisle. I know that for a fact."

Blanca playfully rolled her eyes, but on the inside she wanted to smack the shit out of Lux. She didn't want to just be the center of attention while she walked down the aisle. She wanted to be the center of attention when Lux walked down the aisle, too. Hell, she wanted to be the fuckin' bride.

"Anyway," Blanca said, changing the subject. "What are you two up to after this?"

Lux's eyes lit up. "Mama and I are going to see the venue and do a final walkthrough before they start setting everything up. I won't see it again until the day of. Do you want to come, B? We would love to have you!"

Blanca cocked her head to the side and looked at Mateo. "You aren't going with, Mat?"

Blanca wasn't going to go if Mateo wasn't going. She wanted to keep tabs on him as much as possible, so she patiently waited for his response before giving her own. Lux replied for him before he could even open his mouth. "B, please. You know he's allergic to anything wedding. It was a miracle he came along for the food tasting, but you know he loves to eat."

"That I do," Blanca mumbled.

Lux heard her response, and her smile faltered slightly as she looked at Blanca. They way she said it was odd to her, but she shook it off and glanced at Mateo. "You sure you don't want to come, papi? Just think about it. We could envision our day together."

Mateo shook his head. There was no way he was going to that venue. It felt too much like his final resting place or some shit. He didn't want to see the place they were to get married in until the day of. Even the rehearsal dinner was going to be held at the Rose mansion. It was supposed to be held at his parent's place… but that was no longer an option. Realizing he could use his parent's death as an out, he replied. "I was thinking about going to see my parent's graves…"

Blanca cut her eyes at him again. She knew that was a crock of shit, but she kept quiet. Lux's eyes softened, and she reached across the table to grab his hand. "I think that's a good idea, papi. You haven't been there since the funeral, have you?"

"Nah," Mateo replied.

Lux nodded. "Get some time in with your parents. There will be plenty of other shit we can get into over the next couple of weeks."

He nodded, relieved that she let him slide on this one. Lux turned to Blanca and asked, "What about you, B? You want to come with me and Mama? Just think of all the daydreaming you can do about your own wedding one day."

Lux giggled, and Blanca joined in, but her laughs were as fake as Nicki Minaj's ass. Lux was always joking around about Blanca and her desire to get married. That shit low key hurt Blanca. She knew she got carried away fantasizing about her wedding day, but what Lux didn't realize were two things. One, she truly wanted to be loved. She wanted to feel that shit Lux's parent's had. She wanted the big house, the family, and the loving husband. She wanted what Lux and Mateo had. The shit was no joke to her. It was her deepest desire. She wasn't lucky enough to know who she was going to marry straight out the fuckin' womb like Lux. When she joked about Blanca and her fantasies about getting married, no matter how innocent the jokes were, it hurt Blanca, which filtered into anger and hatred. To her, it was like teasing a woman who couldn't get pregnant about wanting a baby. The shit was that deep. The second thing Lux didn't understand was that when Blanca was daydreaming about her wedding day, she was daydreaming about *her* man. In Blanca's mind, her wedding day would be sooner than anyone thought and with the man she was currently sitting across from. That thought caused a smirk to form on her pretty face before she finally replied to Lux. "I have to pass, too. I have some errands to run for Aunt Dalia."

Lux's pretty face formed into a pout. "Alright. Mama and I will have to make do."

Blanca didn't reply, and a few moments later, a server was at their table, ready to take their orders. They ordered the family platter, which comprised a plethora of their favorite foods, including ropa vieja, yuca, Arroz y Frijoles Negros, echon Asado, and much more. They'd been coming to this restaurant since they were kids, and when they were old enough, they started getting the family platter to share, even though it was entirely too much food for the three of them. Mateo and Lux always sent the leftovers home with Blanca because Dalia loved this place just as much as they did, and she would eat on the leftover food for days. It never went to waste.

When the server finally walked away, Blanca turned to Mateo and asked, "So, how was that work trip you just took?"

He almost spit out the water the server sat down in front of him moments ago, but again, he kept his cool. He swallowed and then pierced her with his dark eyes. "It was cool. Nothing major."

Lux scrunched up her face, and she looked at Blanca. "I don't remember telling you he was going out of town for business."

Blanca froze but quickly recovered. "You didn't. I called him while he was away, and he told me."

Lux frowned even further before she looked at Mateo. "You didn't answer any of my calls."

Mateo squirmed in his seat and had to refrain from kicking Blanca in the fuckin' shin. "She caught me at the right time, and I only talked to her for like a minute, mami. Besides, I'm back now and all yours for the next few weeks."

Lux thought about it for a moment and relaxed. She was slightly annoyed that he had been unreachable for her but had talked to Blanca, but she chalked it up to timing. She decided to let that shit go because they had a wedding they needed to focus on.

"And then you will have him for the honeymoon,

Lux. I bet that shit is going to be *killer*," Blanca chimed in, trying to smooth things over.

This time, Mateo did kick Blanca under the table, but she didn't even flinch while Lux smiled and replied, "You're right about that."

While Lux fantasized about their honeymoon, Blanca did, too. She thought about how her dreams would come true if she could bust up their honeymoon and put a bullet straight through Lux's head. Mateo, on the other hand, watched as the two women in his life seemed to disappear into themselves. He wondered what the fuck they were each thinking about as he sat in a pool of dread.

The next day, Blanca was at work in a foul ass mood. She always was when she was forced to put on her customer service face and serve other mothafuckas, some shit Lux never had to do a day in her life.

Blanca fought the urge to roll her eyes into the back of her head as she listened to a customer complain about their room.

"There were roaches!" he fumed, and Blanca only half listened because she knew this man was lying his ass off. This hotel was as bougie as they got, and she knew for a fact she had never seen a roach her entire time working for the company.

She gave the chubby, balding man a once over. She knew his type. He was a wannabe. There wasn't a designer label on him, and she remembered the woman he checked in with. She had labels dripping from her. She smirked because that woman was nowhere to be seen at the moment. She was no doubt in that expensive ass room ordering room service on his dime. Homeboy was no doubt feeling how light his pockets were messing with a gold digger, and so he was now in Blanca's face, trying to get his room comped.

Her glazed over eyes peered at him as he finally came up for air from his five minute long rant. "Sir, there are no refunds—"

"Where is your manager?" he demanded, and she sighed.

"I am the manager, sir, and when you checked in, you signed documents that stated that you under-stood there were no refunds. I know for a fact we do not have roaches, but if you would like, I can offer you a credit for the spa."

The man glared at her. "This is unbelievable. What kind of establishment is this, anyway?"

"One you clearly can't afford," Blanca mumbled.

"What was that?" the man snapped, and Blanca actually did roll her eyes this time.

"Look, if you want to cut your stay short, we can do that and offer a refund for the days you will not be staying with us, but the three nights already spent here will be charged. Since this place is such a dump,

I am sure your lady friend is dying to leave," Blanca said smoothly.

At the mention of his companion, the man straightened up, and his entire attitude changed out of fear of being kicked out for being rude. He didn't want to disappoint his lady friend, so he sighed heavily and asked, "Spa credit, you said?"

Blanca smirked and tapped away on her computer for a second before returning her gaze to the man. "Two hundred dollars. Just go there and give them your room number. They will be able to pull the credit up and explain what services they can offer you."

The man pursed his chapped lips before grunting and waddling away. Thankfully, the lobby was now empty, and Blanca had a moment to breathe. She hated this job more than anything, but she reminded herself that it wouldn't be too much longer having to deal with this shit.

She pulled out her cellphone from underneath the counter and noticed she had a text from her aunt. She smiled. Dalia was truly a soft spot for Blanca. As hateful and coldhearted as she was toward everyone else, that shit melted away when it came to her aunt.

Dalia: *I hope you are having a good day, mija. I'm making your favorite for dinner.*

Blanca smiled before tapping out another text.

Don't cook tonight. We have leftovers in the fridge from Victors.

Dalia: *I wondered what all those containers were. Thank Lux for me.*

Blanca rolled her eyes at that and decided not to respond. The fact that her aunt automatically assumed Lux was the one that paid for that food pissed her off. Of course, she was right, but still. It was as if Dalia thought Blanca was some broke ass bitch that couldn't afford food or something. While she fumed, she didn't notice the object of her anger walk into the lobby.

"What has your face all balled up, chica?" Lux asked as she approached the counter with a smile. Her long hair was down and flowing, and even her lazy clothes looked like they belonged in a fucking GQ magazine. Today, she was wearing a tan colored Versace jumpsuit. The hoodie was a crop top that showed off her huge breasts, and she was looking as pretty as ever.

Blanca fixed her face into a smile and pushed her anger down. "Lux, what are you doing here?"

Lux reached the counter and held up a plastic bag. "Papa and I had lunch at the place we like around the corner. I thought you might want something, so here I am."

Always so motherfucking thoughtful, Blanca thought.

It wasn't random for Lux to pop up with food for Blanca while she was at work. She was known for doing this shit, and it irritated Blanca. Still, she was going to eat the food. She had been in such a rush that morning that she forgot to pack a lunch. She knew she could have had Mateo drop her off some food, which was what she planned on doing, but she hadn't had a moment to text him. Of course, Lux was here to save the fucking day.

"That's why you texted asking if I was at work?" Blanca asked, recalling the text from earlier in her shift.

"Yup." Lux smiled. "When can you take your break? I figured I could sit with you while you eat. I don't have shit else going on today."

"So… I'm your last resort type shit?" Blanca asked with her nose turned up. She hated how Lux always seemed to be so busy and important. Meanwhile, Blanca was stuck at this stupid ass job getting cursed out by men twice her age.

"Huh? No, B. You know that's never the case… I could always go home and cuddle up with Mat, but I wanted to come check you out. You okay, girl?"

Lux's response only pissed Blanca off even further, but she knew she needed to fix her attitude, so she sighed and came up with a lie. "Yeah, chica. I'm sorry. I'm on my period, so I'm just crabby."

Lux smiled. "I feel you, sis. Thankfully, mine won't come until after the honeymoon. Whew! Could you imagine if I got it during?"

Lux giggled, but Blanca did not. Instead, she opened up her mouth to tell Lux a lie about being the only one there, so she couldn't take a lunch break, but the general manager chose that moment to walk by after being MIA all morning. The bubbly woman smiled at Lux and greeted her. "Lux, it's good to see you. What brings you by?"

Lux smiled. "Hey, Mary. Just dropping off some sandwiches. I brought extras in case you were in today."

Mary beamed. "You know I love it when you come by."

The two giggled, and Blanca clenched her teeth while she watched as Mary dug around in the bag and grabbed a foil wrapped Cuban sandwich and asked Lux about the wedding.

Blanca was forced to listen to their small talk for a few minutes before Mary turned to her and said, "Go ahead and take your lunch. I'll cover for you until you get back."

"Don't you want to eat? I can—"

Mary waved her off. "Nonsense. Spend time with your friend. I'll be here until you get back."

Blanca wanted to groan in protest, but she simply

grasped the plastic bag and made her way around the counter. As soon as she was near enough, Lux looped her arm through hers and guided her outside to the courtyard where a picnic area was. They got situated at a table, and Lux smiled up at the sun while Blanca looked at her in disgust. The bitch always seemed to take pleasure in everything around her, and it irritated Blanca.

By the time Lux was finished basking in the sun, Blanca was digging into her sandwich. She couldn't help but moan in satisfaction. Cuban sandwiches were her favorite, and Lux knew it.

"Good, huh?"

"You already know it," Blanca replied honestly.

"Papa ate two." Lux giggled. She and her dad rarely spent time together outside of some type of assassin shit, so she loved when they took time to do normal things, just the two of them. They were some of her favorite moments.

"I don't know how he does that," Blanca replied fondly. She wasn't even putting up a front. She truly cared about Lux's parents. They were good people in her eyes, and growing up, she always fantasized about them being her own parents. She often wondered why she got the absentee parents while Lux got the coolest parents on the block. The shit was completely unfair. Lux truly had it all, and Blanca believed she didn't even realize it.

Lux shrugged with a smile before she asked, "Sooo, how is Mr. Bae doing? You gonna bring him to the wedding or what?"

Oh, he'll be there alright, Blanca thought, but she shook her head and said, "I'm not ready for him to meet everyone just yet."

Lux cocked her head to the side, her long hair falling over her shoulder. "How's that work, B? You gave him your body, but aren't ready to introduce him to your family and friends?"

Lux was genuinely asking because she had no idea how that logic made sense. To her, sex was a big deal and some shit you only did with someone you loved. She couldn't imagine giving her pussy up to a man she couldn't bring home to her parents.

Blanca scoffed. "It's not even like that, Lux. Sex really isn't even that big of a deal. A lot of people have sex with others that they wouldn't want around their family and friends. It's not that deep."

"Understood," Lux replied, instantly backing off. The last thing she wanted to do was insult Blanca. She was genuinely curious about her logic, but she could tell it made her friend uncomfortable, so she was going to drop it. Blanca was always testy around her cycle time, so she didn't take any offense. In fact, she made a mental note to drop off some chocolates and shit to her at some point this week. That was just the kind of friend Lux was.

"Not everyone is Virgin Mary like you, Lux," Blanca snapped, still annoyed.

Lux smirked. "Now that's where you're wrong, B. I might not be fucking, but Mat and I do a lil' somethin'."

Blanca perked up at that. "Like what?"

As far as she knew, she was the only one fucking, sucking, and jerking Mateo, so to hear this was a bit of a shock.

Lux giggled. "Since you don't want to go into detail about your boy toy, I won't go into detail about mine, but we get intimate in our own ways. The shit be feeling good, too, but I can't wait to get the full experience in a couple of weeks."

The smile on Lux's face was pissing Blanca off. She wanted to smack it off her face, but she stamped that anger down and smiled back at her. "Fair enough. What all do you have planned for the week?"

She changed the subject, but not before making a mental note to talk to Mateo about these intimate moments he'd been having with Lux. Here Blanca thought she was the only one to ever have him in that way, and of course, Lux had to go and take that from her, too. It infuriated her. She angrily took a bite of her sandwich as she listened to Lux.

"We have Mateo's tux fitting in a couple of days, the flowers are getting here on Friday, I have to go shopping for a few things for the honeymoon Saturday…"

Blanca tuned Lux out while she focused on her lunch. When she finally finished talking, Blanca asked, "Is Mat going to be helping with any of that stuff?"

Lux nodded. "As much as I can talk him into. He'll for sure be there when we get his tux fitted because he has no choice. There's no way I'm allowing him to sit around at home while I'm running around like a chicken with my head cut off. So yeah, he will be helping as much as I can get him to."

"Let me know how I can help, too," Blanca replied as she finished off her sandwich.

Lux smiled. "Thanks, chica. You know I will."

Blanca stood from her seat and gave Lux a smile she thought looked genuine. She was over this entire encounter and would rather be back working and dealing with customers than be in Lux's face being fake. "I'm going to head back. Thanks again for lunch."

Lux stood as well and walked around the table

before embracing Blanca. "Of course, B. I hope you feel better. Try a heating pack when you get home. You know that always helps."

Blanca rolled her eyes as she patted Lux's back before pulling away. One thing about Lux was she paid attention to those she loved, and it drove Blanca crazy. The fucking golden child. "Thanks, Lux."

"Any time," Lux replied before winking and walking off.

Blanca watched as she went to the parking lot and got into her Maybach. When she was finally out of sight, the fake smile fell off her face and was replaced with a scowl. She could not wait until this entire wedding ordeal was over with so she could officially be rid of little miss perfect.

"Papa, I can't believe you fucked up your shoulder days before my wedding," Lux grumbled as she helped her father into his suit jacket.

She, Mateo, and Waylan were at the tailors, doing the last fitting for their tuxes. Before they stopped here, Lux stopped by the boutique her dress was being held and grabbed it, since it was officially ready and no more fittings needed to be done. The dress was in her car while they handled the tuxes, and Lux was eager to get it home.

"Mija, enough," Waylan grumbled as he looked at himself in the mirror in front of him. He had been crabby enough as it was.

Mateo stepped out of the dressing room in his white tuxedo, and Lux's eyes swiftly moved up and down his body with lust filling them as he spoke.

"Chaparrita, give your old man a break. He can't help that he pulled a muscle while lifting weights. You aren't helping by your constant nagging."

"That's right. Thank you, Mateo," Waylan appraised before eying his daughter in the mirror.

Lux lifted a perfectly arched brow and shook her head. The truth was, he fucked up his shoulder when he was out of town on yet another job. It was like every gangster and thug in the US suddenly needed someone dead because calls had been coming in left and right. Waylan had already been on three hits, but the last one left him in a fucked up position. The truth was, he was getting old, and there was a reason he didn't take on jobs anymore. One man he was hired to kill got the upper hand on him, and in the struggle, he dislocated his shoulder. Waylan managed to get the job done still, but for a minute he feared he had met his end.

When he came home in a sling, both Dionne and Lux made a huge fuss over him, and that only made him crabbier. Lux was trying to keep her slick comments at bay, but she was honestly worried about her father. It was just an injured shoulder, but it could have been much worse, and that was something Mateo didn't understand because he only knew the cover-up story.

Before Lux could put her future husband in his

place, a familiar voice called out, "Que pasa, familia?"

Lux turned, and a smile formed on her face when she spotted Blanca walking toward them. Mateo swore under his breath, so nobody else heard him. Blanca had been on him like white on rice the past few days, and the shit was making him anxious. It seemed like she was popping up everywhere he was, and he was nervous Lux was going to catch on. So far, she hadn't because she was so wrapped up in wedding shit, and then her pops got injured, which left her tending to him. In a terrible way, he was thankful Waylan got hurt because it left him free to deal with Blanca's erratic ass.

"What are you doing here, chica?" Lux asked, giving Blanca a hug.

"I remembered you saying you were getting their tuxes today, so I thought I would stop by," Blanca replied.

Lux's brow furrowed. "I didn't tell you what time, though."

Blanca kept a smile on her face, but inside she was kicking herself. She noticed Lux had been catching her ass in more lies lately, and she knew she needed to tighten up. "Lucky guess. I was just out riding around and thought I would swing by and see if y'all were here."

Mateo eyed her. He wondered how her ass knew they were here, too. He hadn't told her what he was doing today because he hadn't had the time to talk to her. Lux had been with him all day, and he planned on touching base with Blanca after he wrapped shit up here.

Blanca gave him a stiff smile. Him not returning her calls or texts all morning had her nervous, especially since Lux hadn't been answering hers, either. She made the executive decision to pop up on them. She had been staking out the tailor's shop for a few hours, waiting for them to arrive. When they did, she continued calling Mateo to see if he would leave the shop so she could run up on him and curse him out for ignoring her, but he didn't answer nor did he come out of the shop, leaving her no other option but to go in. She was relived to see that shit was normal, and it didn't look like Mateo fucked things up for her and the plan she so desperately needed to execute.

"You could have called to ask," Lux pointed out, still confused by Blanca's reasoning.

Blanca cocked her head to the side. "I did. Both of you."

She discreetly cut her eyes at Mateo, who looked like a deer in headlights. He hadn't gotten any calls because both he and Lux left their phones at home that morning. He gestured toward Lux and said, "Talk to ya girl."

Lux giggled. "My bad, B. I forgot we left our phones at home this morning. I didn't want any distractions today. I damn near had to pry Mat's phone from his hand, but I got my way in the end. We had a nice breakfast, and we took Papa to his dctor appointment for his shoulder before coming here."

Blanca nodded slowly, relieved that was what happened and not anything else that could have fucked things up for her. She looked at Waylan and smiled. "And how are you, Mr. Rose? What happened to your shoulder?"

"Don't ask," he grumbled before opening his good arm up to Blanca. She walked into his embrace, and when they pulled apart, he asked, "How are you? How's Dalia?"

"I'm fine, and Dalia is the same as ever. Stubborn and a nag," Blanca said with a giggle, but everyone knew she was just talking. She loved her aunt.

"She needs to find a good man," Waylan said with a chuckle of his own. "I have a few associates I can hook her up with, and she knows it, too. When she's ready to settle down and be treated right, tell her to call me, and I'll hook her up."

Blanca playfully bumped Waylan's good shoulder. "Now you know that will never happen."

Mateo watched as Blanca interacted with Waylan. He knew she really cared for Lux's parents, but he couldn't understand how she could love them but knowingly want to kill their daughter. Blanca was complex, and that was what originally drew him in. Now, he felt like she just left his ass confused, and he wasn't wrong.

"Speaking of settling down and being treated right… Blanca has a secret man," Lux said playfully.

Blanca's eyes grew wide while Mateo choked on his own spit. Lux giggled at Mateo and patted him on the back. "I know, papi. I was just as shocked as you."

"Who is this young man?" Waylan asked as he peered at Blanca.

"Nobody you know," she said swiftly. "It isn't that serious. Lux doesn't know what she is talking about."

Before Lux could tease her friend any further, a chime sounded from her purse. Mateo's thick brows drew in as he asked, "What the fuck was that?"

Lux looked at him guiltily before going to her purse and pulling her work phone out of it. "It's work, Mat—"

"Aw, hell nah. You begged me to leave my shit at

the house while you still had your phone on you? How is that fair? I thought today was supposed to be distraction free?" Mateo ranted.

He had already been annoyed when Lux insisted they go through the day without their phones because he knew Blanca would freak, which was probably why she tracked his ass down. To make matters worse, he couldn't even warn Blanca before Lux pulled the phone away from him and marched him out the door. To find out she still had her work phone on her had him pissed. He knew when that shit chimed, it meant Lux was about to be MIA. He hated that fuckin' phone. He had never met a woman that was so dedicated to her work, and the entire operation was so secretive. It drove him nuts.

"I promise I didn't know anything work-related would come through. You know I carry my work phone with me everywhere—"

"Like I carry my phone with me? I don't have a separate line for work and personal, so again, how is this fair?" Mateo asked.

Lux looked down at the phone in her hand and read the text.

Atlanta. Terry Abrams. Make that shit messy. Send pics. End of the week.

Another chime notified her that a wire had been sent through. She sighed before looking at Mateo with sad eyes. "Papi, it's not fair, and I'm sorry, okay? But you know I never ignore work. Ever. It's a definite rule that I can't break."

"I thought you took the next few weeks off," Mateo replied with a scowl on his face. He glanced at Waylan and said, "I thought he was taking over—"

"Mat, Papa is injured. He can't handle the job right now. He needs to rest," Lux replied calmly. She felt terrible because she knew she was going back on some promises she made to him, but there wasn't much that could be done. Work was work... period. She was trained to never miss an assignment, and she wouldn't start now because Mateo was having a tantrum.

"He doesn't need his arm to handle business, Lux," Mateo replied. Lux shook her head. If only he knew. She knew there was no way Waylan could handle another job. Not with his shoulder fucked up, and she wasn't sure he should ever do another job again. Last time had been the first time in his life he had been touched, and that scared Lux. He was invincible to her, so the entire thing wasn't sitting right with her. It was proof that her parents were aging. They weren't grandparents or anything like that, but they were slowing down in what they could and could not do, and that was something she wasn't ready to face.

She glanced at her father, who had a hard look on his face. She knew he wasn't happy with the way Mateo was behaving, so to smooth things over, she stepped to Mateo and wrapped her arms around him. "Papi, please. You have to understand. He can't go. I have to do this. I promise to be back in just a few days… sooner if I can."

Mateo scoffed and stepped out of her embrace. Without saying another word, he walked out of the shop with the Tuxedo on and everything. Lux felt bad, but she wasn't for the disrespect or the embarrassment, so her temper flared just that quick. A flash of her cutting off one of his ugly ass toes fleeted through her mind before she took a deep breath.

"Let me go knock some damn sense into his ass," Lux seethed as she made a move for the door.

Waylan stopped her with his good arm and said, "No, let me."

Blanca stepped in and stopped Waylan, seeing that the older man was upset. "Both of you need to chill. I'll go get Mat and bring him home, okay? That will give everyone time to cool down. You guys finish up here, and I'll call you later, Lux."

Blanca gave each of them a hasty hug before leaving. Waylan and Lux looked at each other.

"You're lucky Blanca stepped in. I was about to put one through his eyes for acting like such a lil' bitch. I don't know how Castillo raised his son, but that was unacceptable. Does he always behave like this?" Waylan asked his daughter.

Lux could see the anger in his eyes, and she wanted to smooth things over. Her parents had only ever seen the calm and collected Mateo. She had known the other side of him for some time now. When he didn't get his way, he was good for talking slick and walking out on her. She had to practice an ample amount of patience dealing with him over the years, but nobody else really knew that.

"Papa, can you blame him? I don't like how he just acted, but he does have every right to be upset."

Waylan looked like he was about to argue with Lux, but she cut him off. "Get changed, and I'll go pay for the tuxes so we can go. I have to text Anthony to get the jet ready, and I'll smooth things over with Mateo back at the house, okay? Don't worry, I'll make sure he gets put in his place."

Lux grinned at her father, and he relaxed slightly. He knew Lux had a way with words and could set a mothafucka straight without raising her voice or even using violence. She got that shit from her mother.

"Fine, but if I see some shit like that again…"

"Papa, it's fine, okay?" she asked, pleading through her eyes for him to drop it.

"Fine," he replied before walking into a dressing room so he could get changed.

Lux sighed and ran a hand through her thick waves as she thought about what the fuck she was going to say to Mateo to smooth things over but also get her point across that he had her entirely fucked up.

L ux looked down at the scattered toes at her feet and absentmindedly sighed. The man groaning in the background did nothing for her. Normally, she would be feeling a certain high after almost completing a job, but she felt anything but. She had been tracking this Terry nigga down for two days. She had to hand it to him… he was a slippery mothafucka who definitely did not want to be found. He even had the resources not to be found… if Lux had been the average person, but she wasn't. She finally found him and had spent the last twelve hours torturing him and sending her client photos along the way, as they requested.

Lux was honestly just over it. She had been annoyed when she couldn't find him right away because all she wanted to do was get home. She hadn't had the chance to see Mateo before she left, and he hadn't answered his phone since. They might go hours without speaking to each other, but this had been a first for her. Going days without hearing from him was driving her crazy. When she texted Blanca, she only got vague responses, which only irritated her more. She knew Blanca was busy with work, but damn. Any time she asked her parents if they had seen Mateo, they said he hadn't been home. Her temper was flaring, and she was doing her best to channel it into Terry, but it wasn't working.

She finally decided she fulfilled her job well enough as she looked around the warehouse. It was one she had been to many times before since Atlanta was a hotspot for her. There was blood covering the plastic that laid on the floor. Terry was in bad shape. She had really done a number on him. Both his ears were missing, various toes, he'd been stabbed repeatedly in places that purposely wouldn't kill him, his fingertips had been burned to a crisp… the list went on. She had been a busy assassin, but her heart was no longer in it.

Without another thought, she picked up a large machete from a bag she brought with her with all the tools she would need for this job. Turning to face Terry, she said, "I think it's time to end this."

Terry didn't respond. He was too far gone to say anything. The fact that Lux had cut his tongue out long ago didn't help, either. He sat looking a bloody mess strapped to the chair by metal chains. His head hung so his chin was hitting his chest, giving Lux the perfect angle to do what she had to do. In one motion, she lifted the machete and brought it down sharply on the back of Terry's neck. The blade was so sharp, it only took one swoop for his head to come clean off.

Lux stared at it as it thudded to the ground at her feet, lost in her thoughts. Mindlessly, she took a phone out of the pocket of the mesh suit she wore to take one final photo. She hit send to her client, then put the burner back into her suit. It would get burned along with her clothing within the next few minutes.

She carefully collected all her items before exiting the building and sending a text to the clean-up crew. As soon as she was stripped down to her normal clothes, and her mesh suit was in the plastic bag in the front seat along with the burner phone, she got in the driver's seat and immediately pulled out her personal phone. The shit was dry as hell. There was only a text from her mother asking her to let her know when she was finished working. She always had a text like that from her mother waiting for her after jobs, so she was sure it was nothing important, but she started up her car and called her mother as requested.

After a few rings, Dionne answered. "Hey, baby. I was getting worried. Long day?"

"Yeah," Lux replied. "It was a long one this time, but I'm heading home soon. Have you seen Mat?"

"No, baby, I haven't," Dionne replied with compassion in her voice. Dionne knew Mateo not coming around was weighing heavily on her daughter, which was why she had been worried. Being distracted like that was a sure way to fuck up on a job and get herself killed. After Waylan's scare last time, Dionne was pretty much at her wit's end.

"Okay, I'm going to try calling him," Lux replied, preparing to get off the phone.

"Do that, but maybe you should spend an extra day in Atlanta. We haven't heard from Reg and Trina lately. Why don't you see if they have some time to get together?" Dionne suggested. She didn't have many friends growing up, but Trinity and Reginald were her for-lifers. They grew up running the same circles, but Dionne was set kind of apart from them because she was a kingpin's daughter, and Trinity and Reginald were trying to make it up out the hood. The two of them worked for her father once they were old enough, but they went to the same school in elementary for a hot second before Dionne was transferred to a private school. She didn't click with all the siditty girls, so she and Trinity stayed tight through the years. The Reigns were the only people who knew her daughter and what she did outside of family, and Dionne wouldn't have it any other way. Truth be told, in the early days, right after she and Waylan married and she found out the true reason behind their arranged marriage, she had ideas to have Lux marry into the Reign family. Unfortunately, fate had other plans, and that idea was shut out. Ultimately, she would have been most comfortable leaving her daughter in the hands of her friends, and they even entertained the idea for a short while before shit changed and that was no longer an option.

Lux thought about what her mother said. The idea had crossed her mind briefly when she first touched down in Atlanta, but she had been so occupied with finding Terry and dealing with Mateo's silence that it slipped her mind. She would feel like shit if she didn't at least reach out to her godparents, since she was in their city. She sighed and said, "You're right, Mama. I will. I'll let you know if I link up with them and when I'm headed home."

"Tell Trina to call me sometime. It's been too long. I know those babies are over there keeping her busy, but I miss my friend," Dionne replied. She recently sent Trinity a text to see if they could set a time and day to catch up on FaceTime, but the text went unanswered.

"I got you, Mama," Lux replied. "Love you."

"I love you too, baby," Dionne responded before disconnecting the call.

Lux navigated the streets easily as she dialed Mateo's number next. It went straight to voicemail, like it had been doing since she touched down in Atlanta. Next, she dialed Blanca to see if her best friend had talked to Mateo, or at least to see if she could talk some sense into him for her, but her phone rang and rang until it went to voicemail. Frustrated, Lux decided to give Trinity a call to help get her mind off Mateo for a second. She truly couldn't understand why he was being such an ass all of a sudden, but she knew they needed to figure that shit out within the next few days, because she refused to get married while shit felt off between them. Arranged marriage or not… she wasn't going to be in a difficult marriage. She wanted that love her parents had. The kind of love Reginald and Trinity had with each other.

Trinity's phone rang once and then an operator connected, saying the line was disconnected. Lux's brows furrowed before she dialed Reginald's phone. His shit only went to voicemail, so she left a message and shrugged her shoulders. It seemed as though she was going home instead of staying a few days. If she was in a better headspace, she might have taken a moment to track the Reign family down, but she wasn't. She was eager to get home and see Mateo face to face, so she pressed her foot down on the pedal and made her way to the Airbnb so she could get the fuck home.

ateo had been drunk for forty-eight hours straight, and Blanca knew he would be feeling it this morning. When he stormed out on Lux and her father at his tux fitting, he immediately felt like shit, but guilt was eating at him, and he was subconsciously looking for reasons to fight with Lux. Possibly even end things with her in order to save her. Then again, he didn't want to let her go, either. There was a constant war within himself, and the only thing that would quiet that shit was tequila.

Instead of having Blanca drop him off at home, he instructed her to take him to their suite at her job. Blanca had been happy to comply. From there, she witnessed him self destruct, but she really didn't care. As long as he was doing it in her company and not anyone else's. She even went as far as to take his phone from him and turn it off. She knew Lux would be calling him, and she didn't want his drunk mind to speak sober thoughts. He wasn't thinking clearly, and she was actually happy to have him all to herself for a little while, since Lux was out of town doing God knows what. Blanca had been the one to plant the seed about Lux cheating every time she went out of town randomly. She felt like that shit was mad sketchy. Mateo was in the drug business and neither he nor his father ever had to leave out of nowhere and were unreachable at times. It was easy for Blanca to plant that seed, and all she had to do was sit back and watch the shit fester.

Now Mateo was passed out next to her, and she was ready to get up and get their day started. She wanted to steer him away from drinking today and just enjoy his company. She wanted to fuck on him and forget about everything else. She wanted to be selfish with him and get a true taste of what life would be like when Lux was out of the picture.

She rolled over and nudged Mateo to wake him up. "Mateo."

He stirred but kept his eyes closed. Blanca kissed her teeth, and with another shove, Mateo's eyes popped open as he looked around wildly, confused and dehydrated. "Huh? Wha—"

"Get up, papi," Blanca whined. "I want to play."

Mateo stared at her for a moment, his hair wild and his eyes dark and hard. Finally, his eyes softened, and he looked around the room once again. There was an empty bottle of tequila on the desk in the corner, and pizza boxes were scattered across the room, along with various takeout containers and empty water bottles. He turned his nose up at the mess and said, "Call housekeeping, B. This shit is disgusting."

Blanca shook her head. "You made this mess, Mat. You call them… shit."

He groaned and asked, "What the fuck happened?"

"Lux had a job." Blanca put her fingers up in air quotes to further plant that seed that she was cheating before continuing, "You stormed out of the tux fitting and demanded I take you here where you proceeded on a two-day drinking binge, and quite frankly, I'm over it and ready to enjoy you. Not drunk you, but my future husband you."

Blanca scooted over to him and kissed his bare chest. Mateo was still doing his best to catch his bearings while she kissed down his body. When she got to the elastic of his briefs, he stopped her and said, "Let me shower and shit first, B. Order us some food so I can soak up this liquor, and clean up some of this mess."

Blanca pouted as he nudged her off him and stood to his feet. He was a bit dizzy, so he took a moment to steady himself before walking toward the bathroom door.

"You really just expect me to do all that before getting any dick?" Blanca spat.

Mateo chuckled. "You're gonna be my wife, right? You should want to take care of me, mami."

Blanca was the queen of mind games, but Mateo knew how to do a lil' somethin', too, and it showed because Blanca immediately perked up. He knew she was always willing to prove herself to be a better wife than Lux could ever be, and he wasn't ashamed to admit that he played on that sometimes. He watched as Blanca got out of bed in all her naked glory and immediately began gathering food containers. He smiled before going into the bathroom to handle his business.

By the time he got out forty-five minutes later, the room was clean, Blanca was dressed, and there was a tray of breakfast foods on the table that sat in the living room portion of the suite. Mateo plopped down next to Blanca at the table and eyed the food. His stomach wasn't really up for eating, but he knew he needed to if he wanted to feel better. Blanca peered over at him and asked, "Feeling better?"

"A little, but my head is killing me. How much

did I drink, anyway?" he asked.

"You don't want to know, papi," Blanca replied as she dished up a plate for him. She sat the food in front of him and said, "Eat. It'll help."

He nodded and begrudgingly picked up a piece of toast. He took a bit and chewed slowly before untwisting the cap of the cold water bottle sitting in front of him and washing the bread down with it. She watched him for a few moments, admiring his handsome features before he spoke and had to ruin the moment for her. "Have you heard from Lux?"

Blanca scrunched her face up. "A little."

He chewed on some eggs and thought about what he wanted to ask next. He finally decided to just fuck it and ask directly what he wanted to know. "Has she asked about me?"

Blanca rolled her eyes. She hated when he asked her about Lux, and he knew it, but he couldn't remember shit about the last few days and needed her to catch him up.

"No, the bitch didn't ask about you," Blanca lied. Lux had most definitely been trying to ask Blanca about Mateo, but she curved her or ignored her because what the fuck did she look like, giving Lux any information about her future husband? Nah, couldn't be her, but Mateo didn't need to know all that. The more he thought Lux was fucking around on him and didn't care about him, the easier the next several days would go for her.

He dropped his fork, his appetite completely gone, as he buried his head in his hands. "What the fuck, man? What the fuck do you think she's doing?"

Blanca shrugged when he glanced at her. "Could be anything."

She was being vague on purpose, but lust, love, and all the other bullshit floating through his head blinded Mateo, so he didn't even pick up on her nonchalance and the fact that she didn't have any real input on the situation. Mateo finally popped his head up and stood to his feet. "I need a drink."

Blanca immediately stood to her feet and placed her hands on his chest. "No, Mat. Not today, papi. I want to actually spend time with you before you have to go back to Lux."

He peered down at her for a moment before brushing past her. "I ain't even sure I'll go back to her."

He walked over to the counter that was situated right next to the kitchenette in the living room and grasped a fresh bottle of tequila. Blanca rushed over to him and stopped him from opening it. "What the fuck do you mean, Mat?"

"Exactly what I said. Lux ain't checking for me. Why the fuck should I marry her?" he asked miserably. He was honestly torn. He wanted to make things right with Lux because he knew he had been acting an ass for a while now, but he also didn't want to leave Blanca. He felt it was probably better for everyone involved if he and Blanca just left and lived their lives away from all the bullshit.

"Because, Mateo," Blanca snapped. "We have a plan. You just need another day or two to clear your head. And no more drinking!"

She snatched the bottle from him and swiftly uncapped it and poured its contents down the drain. It was the last bottle, so unless he left to get more, which she wasn't going to let him, he was ass out of luck if he wanted to drink.

"Really, B? Why—"

Blanca didn't give him the chance to say shit else or start an argument. She walked over to him and dropped to her knees before unbuckling his belt and freeing his semi-hard dick. One thing about Mateo, he was always turned on when in her presence, whether he was even aware of it or not. It didn't matter because Blanca always knew.

She put his thick dick inside her warm mouth, and Mateo immediately forgot what he was upset about in the first place. She had that power over him. He looked down at her as she worked up enough spit to wet his entire dick, including his balls. Blanca was messy when it came to sex, head included, and he loved that shit.

He watched as her hand disappeared up her sundress, and seconds later, he could hear her wetness as she played with her pussy.

"Fuck, Blanca," he groaned as she suctioned his dick like a pro.

He was feeling good, but he wanted to feel her pussy, so he pulled away from her and pulled her up, grabbing hold of the hand that had been playing in her pussy. Blanca watched as he sucked her slender fingers into his mouth and moaned.

"Taste good, papi?" she asked, already knowing the answer.

"Hell yeah," he replied before turning her around and lifting her blue sundress. As he expected, she didn't have any panties on, and Mateo wasted no time bending her over. Blanca smiled as she hung on to the counter in the kitchenette and looked back at her lover. She smirked when she saw him rubbing the head of his dick at her wet opening.

"Stop playing and fuck me, Mateo," Blanca pleaded, and Mateo complied.

He pushed the head in, and both he and Blanca sighed in satisfaction. That right there was exactly what they needed. Sex was where they thrived and bonded the most. It was therapy for them, and while they were consumed by each other in that way, everything else was forgotten.

"Fuck," Mateo groaned as he slid in even further.

Blanca moaned in response as she threw her ass back, silently begging him for more. Mateo complied. He wrapped his large hand around her middle and pulled her into him repeatedly. Blanca was standing on her tiptoes and barely able to catch her balance as Mateo pounded into her with no mercy. The only sound that could be heard was their skin smacking together.

Blanca's legs shook as she felt an orgasm building up in the core of her stomach. "Mat, I'm close."

"So am I, mami," Mateo gritted out as he concentrated on his pacing. He could feel Blanca's pussy gripping his dick repeatedly, and he knew she was about to bust. He watched in anticipation, and it didn't take long for juices to seep onto his dick, down his balls, and on his thighs.

"Ahhh," Blanca moaned in pure bliss. Mateo had a way of making her feel like she was floating. The only thing she almost wanted more than Lux's downfall was life with Mateo's dick. *Almost.* Still, she was crazy over his dick and possessive. She had yet to confront him about the little tidbit Lux told her about how they were sexual in their own way, but she would when the time was right.

Moments later, Mateo pulled out and jerked his dick a few times before he was spilling his seed on Blanca's back. "Damn."

"I can't wait until you can fill me up with that cum of yours, Mateo," Blanca breathed seductively.

Mateo smacked her ass and then went into the bathroom to get her a towel without responding. He couldn't wait to have kids one day as well. The problem was, he could never envision if those kids would be Lux's or Blanca's.

He walked out of the bathroom with a towel, dick swinging and all. Blanca smiled at the sight before he got behind her to clean up her back. When he finished, he tossed the soiled towel on the ground and turned Blanca around. He pressed his forehead to hers and said, "You're the only one truly in my corner."

Blanca beamed up at him. That was exactly what she wanted him to feel. Mission accomplished. She leaned up to kiss him before pulling away and saying, "Take a couple of days to get your head right, Mat, and then let's finish this thing, eh?"

After a moment of contemplation, Mateo nodded, and Blanca smiled up at him adoringly. She was so fucking close to getting everything she wanted. It was only a matter of time before everything came together for her.

L ux had been calling Mateo since she got off the plane. His fucking phone was going straight to voicemail, and his mailbox was full because she had been leaving messages left and right. She navigated the streets toward Blanca's house to get some answers. Blanca wasn't answering her phone, either, but at least Lux knew where Blanca lived and could pop up on her. She called her mom when she got off the plane and was informed that Mateo still hadn't been home, so she had no idea where to even start looking for his ass. Don't get it twisted… she could easily find him, but she had never crossed those lines with her family and friends because she wanted to respect their privacy, so she was trying hard to uphold that.

She finally pulled into Blanca's home and got out of her car. Dalia was outside in her garden, and when she noticed Lux, she smiled and waved at the younger woman.

"What brings you here, mija?" Dalia asked as she stood and walked over to Lux to greet her.

After a brief hug, Lux replied, "I was just coming to see Blanca. I can't seem to get ahold of her, and I'm trying to find Mat. He and I got into a fight the other day, and I haven't seen him since, so I wanted to see if B has heard from him."

Dalia's eyes softened. "Blanca isn't here, mija. She is with her invisible boyfriend."

"Invisible boyfriend?" Lux asked, and then covered her mouth to giggle. "What do you mean?"

Dalia shrugged. "I've never met the boy. She only talks about him briefly and says when the time is right, she will bring him around."

Lux nodded with a smile. "Yeah, that's about all I know, too." She sighed before asking. "That means you don't know where he lives?"

Dalia shook her head. "No. She stays gone for days at a time sometimes with him and then comes back here as if nothing has happened. When I try to dig for information, she clams up. I tell you she's as stubborn as they come."

Lux giggled. "Yeah, she definitely is private. Okay, well, thanks anyway."

Lux turned to leave, but Dalia stopped her. "You

said you and Mateo got into a fight... was it serious, Lux? I hate to think of you two fighting so close to the wedding."

Lux faced the older woman and offered her a warm smile. "Don't you start worrying. We will be fine once we sit down and talk. He's another one that can be stubborn, but it's nothing I can't handle."

Dalia looked at her with her brows wrinkled, but she decided not to press her. She knew how passionate Lux was about Mateo, and she didn't want to seem like a nagging old lady, but something in her spirit told her that if Lux ended up marrying Mateo, it would be bad news for her. Instead, the older woman grasped Lux's hands and said, "I love you, mija. I think of you as a daughter, just as I do Blanca. I just always want you to be happy."

"And I will be," Lux replied with a smiled. "Do you need anything? Food? Do you need me to take you anywhere? Anything like that?"

Dalia shook her head and patted Lux's cheek. "Always such a sweet girl. No, Lux. This old lady is just fine. Go home and get some sleep, eh? You look tired."

Lux realized she was definitely tired, so she nodded her head and said, "I think I'll do just that. Have a good night, Ms. Dalia."

"You too, mija," Dalia replied with a wave before Lux turned and got back into her car.

Once she was safely out of the driveway, she dialed Mateo again and blew out a breath of frustration when his voicemail picked up. She had no other choice but to head home and wait for him to appear, so she did just that.

"Lux, I thought you were staying in Atlanta another day or so," Dionne said when she spotted her daughter in the dining room doorway with her work bag in her hands.

Lux sighed and plopped down in a chair next to her father, dropping her bag at her feet. "I tried getting ahold of Trinity and Reginald, but they didn't answer. I think Trinity got a new phone or something."

"Hmm… I'll have to try calling her later," Dionne replied. "I've sent her a few messages but haven't gotten a response."

"Yeah, I'm not sure what's up. Definitely try calling them. Let me know if you need me to find them," Lux replied with a shrug.

"That won't even be necessary, killa," Dionne said with a giggle before waving her daughter off.

"What's wrong, nena?" Waylan asked as he watched Lux rest her head in her hands. As always, he was out of the loop when it came to Lux and her everyday life. If it was about a job, he and Lux would spend hours talking about that shit, but anything else, he didn't even think to ask. It was just how their relationship was set up, but the way Lux was looking now, he knew something was up, and his first concern was always that the two women in his life were okay.

"I haven't spoken to Mateo since the tux fitting, Papa. I don't know what to do," Lux replied.

"Find his ass and—"

"No, that isn't always the answer, Waylan," Dionne said before popping her husband on the back of the head because she already knew what he was going to say. Using their training to handle family and friends was a big no-no in Dionne's book, and she implemented that rule very early on for the both of them. She didn't care if it was just to find someone. She believed in showing the people they loved the respect to move freely without always being watched.

"Maybe he's right, Mama. I mean, the wedding is in just over a week... I can't go too much longer without speaking to him, or we will have to call the wedding off," Lux replied.

Dionne sighed. "I think Mateo will show up before it gets to that point. Give him a little longer and think about what you want to say to him when you see him. Maybe a nice long talk is needed to see if this wedding is even worth going through with."

"Of course, it's worth it," Waylan replied. "Mateo just needs to stop being a pussy and—"

Dionne slapped the back of Waylan's head once again before looking at her daughter. "Just think about what I said."

There was a war going on inside Lux. She agreed with both her parents, honestly. She wished both options were workable and didn't contradict each other, but unfortunately, that wasn't the case, so she sighed and said, "Yes, Mama."

"Good. Do you want some dinner? I can make you a plate," Dionne asked as she gestured toward the plates in front of her and Waylan. They'd just sat down to dinner when Lux came into the room.

"No, that's okay. You two enjoy. I'm just going to go to bed. It's been a long few days," Lux replied before standing up and waving to her parents.

"Get some rest, baby," Dionne replied.

"I will," Lux said, before grabbing her bag and exiting the room. She made her way slowly through the mansion in deep thought, wondering what her next move was going to be. Something just didn't feel right to her, and it was bothering her. She didn't like feeling so unsettled.

When she got to her room, she dropped her bag next to the door and stripped out of her clothing. She grabbed her phone out of her purse and looked at it. The shit was dry as hell… not a single text or phone call from anyone.

Somberly, she walked over to her bed and collapsed in it before plugging her phone into the charger that sat on her nightstand. She made sure her volume was up so she would hear the phone go off before rolling over and staring out the balcony window and door. Lux contemplated her predicament as her eyes became heavy. Finally, just before her eyes closed and sleep overtook her, she decided in the morning she would track Mateo if she hadn't heard him. That way, she was honoring her mother by giving him more time, but also following the instinct her father gave her if he decided not to show up. Either way, by tomorrow afternoon, she would have some answers, and that was enough to allow her to fall into a peaceful slumber.

Blanca stared at the TV in the bedroom of the hotel suite as it played some show Mateo was into. They had been hugged up all day, and it was getting late into the night. The comments Lux made the other day about her and Mateo being intimate were bothering her. She had been trying to keep a clear head all day and keep Mateo distracted from thinking about Lux, but she was exhausted now, which allowed her mind to wander. Finally, she lifted her head from Mateo's bare chest and looked at him. "Mat, have you and Lux had sex?"

Mateo's thick eyebrows furrowed as he looked down at Blanca. "Why would you even ask that? You know she's a virgin."

"Well... have you two done anything besides kiss?"

Mateo shifted uncomfortably. Talking about his sex life with Lux with Blanca was not high on his list of priorities. Hell, it wasn't a priority for him at all. What Mateo and Lux shared was sacred. There were some things he just didn't want to share with Blanca, and this was one of them.

"Where is all this coming from?" he asked.

"The other day she mentioned y'all have done some shit… I just want to know what exactly that is," Blanca admitted as she stared into Mateo's eyes, trying to gauge his reaction.

Mateo let out a deep breath. "We haven't done much. We do… play with each other, though."

"Play with each other? Mateo, come on. We aren't six. What the fuck does that even mean?" Blanca snapped.

He shook his head. "I don't get why you would want to even know this."

"Because I thought I was the only one to have ever seen your dick, and now you're telling me that isn't true," Blanca said with a deep frown on her face.

"I never told you that, though. I never lied to you—"

"I assumed. Sue me. I thought Lux was too prudish to even look at a dick, let alone know what to do with one. So… what? You guys give each other head or something?" she asked.

He shook his head again. "No, we've never done that, but she will jack me off, and I'll play in her pussy… shit like that."

Blanca laughed, but it was more in anger than anything. "So juvenile."

Mateo shrugged. "Compared to what we do… it is juvenile as hell, but that's as far as she was willing to go."

"And you couldn't turn her simple ass down?" Blanca asked with an attitude. She didn't like the thought of Mateo and Lux doing anything sexual, no matter how childish it seemed. It pissed her off that Lux had gotten those intimate moments with her man. Yet another reason for her to put a bullet in her head.

Mateo laughed. "We started doing that shit when we were young. A horny teenager wasn't about to turn that shit down."

"Okay, but I was throwing pussy at you since we were young… who gave you your first sexual encounter?" Blanca asked.

"You. But my first kiss was with her," he replied honestly. "Why does this shit matter, anyway? Lux doesn't give a fuck about me, and it's you I'm going to end up with. Who gives a fuck?"

He pulled Blanca into him and kissed her. She tried resisting at first, but melted into him eventually.

He was hard to resist, even when she wanted to, but in the back of her mind she was still hot about what she just found out. It was a good thing she hadn't asked these questions sooner, because living with this knowledge for years while Lux was still living would have been pure torture. Days, though… that she could handle easily.

A knock at the door startled Lux out of her sleep. Her eyes popped open, and she glanced at the digital clock on her nightstand. It was seven in the morning. She had been asleep longer than usual, but that was okay. She figured she probably needed that rest for the day that was ahead. Since Mateo hadn't shown up or even texted her, she knew she was going to be tracking his ass down today, which meant there would be a confrontation. She didn't know what the resolution would be, but she knew they needed to talk either way.

Rubbing the sleep out of her eyes, she called out, "Come in!"

A second later, Dionne came through the door with a smile on her face. Lux already knew she was up to something if she was in her room this early in the morning. She rarely came to the third floor, so this shit was already suspicious to Lux.

"Good morning," Dionne sang.

"Good morning, Mama. What's up?" Lux asked with her brow raised.

Dionne perched at the end of Lux's bed and smiled at her daughter. "I was thinking we could have a mother daughter day, just the two of us. You know… something before the wedding because after you'll be busy being a wife and giving me grandkids."

Lux rolled her eyes. There was the talk about her having kids… something everyone assumed she wanted but never really asked. She didn't want to comment on that with her mother at the moment, though. Instead, she said, "If the wedding is even happening."

Dionne nodded. "And if it doesn't, then that will not be the end of the world, baby."

"Are you sure, Mama? I have been trained my entire life to marry Mateo… I just can't understand why things are going left with us all of a sudden and right before the wedding. I can't picture my life without him, but I also can't picture being in a marriage with him acting out like this every other day." Lux swiped a hand through her mangled hair and blew out a frustrated breath. She loved Mateo.

Anyone with eyes could see that, but she was raised to be a strong woman. Someone who took care of herself and knew her boundaries. Mateo was really testing her, and both Dionne and Waylan hated to see it. Everyone assumed he was acting out because his parents died and now he didn't know what the fuck to do with his life, but they couldn't be sure because he was refusing to talk to anyone. He was hot one minute and cold the next. Nobody wanted to put up with that shit, so he needed to pull himself together, and fast.

"When you get the chance to talk to him, do your best to get to the root of his problem. If it's the job stuff he's really worried about, do your best to smooth that over if you really love him and want to marry him. Once the wedding is over, you can come clean, and he will have a better understanding. If he refuses to get back to the Mateo you've loved your entire life… then do what is best for you, Lux. There are other kingpins out there to help your career survive. You can find one and naturally fall in love if it comes to that. You don't need Mateo. It's about if you want him or not at this point since the contract with his parents is void."

Lux let her other's words sink in before she got out of bed and made it up, working her way around her mother. When she was finished, she turned to

Dionne and said, "Let's go have breakfast by the beach, but when we are finished, I am tracking Mateo down. I don't have time to play with his ass, and I need answers now. You aren't slick. I know this girl's day was your idea to stall me from crossing that line and tracking him down."

Dionne giggled and put her hands up in mock surrender. "You got me. Maybe during breakfast I can change your mind. Go ahead and get dressed, baby. I'll whip something up for breakfast."

Dionne got up, and Lux watched as her mother walked out of the room and closed her door. She sighed heavily before stepping into the bathroom so she could relieve her bladder and take a hot ass shower. It didn't take her long to get clean before she was running a brush through her thick mane and throwing her hair into a messy bun at the top of her head. Next, she went to her closet and slipped on a pair of biker shorts and a crop top, deciding that she wasn't going to actually get in the water that morning. She knew her mother was going to try to prolong their breakfast, but Lux's stomach was in knots, and truthfully, she just wanted to find Mateo and get the shit over with. On top of that, her anxiety was mounting that maybe something was actually wrong with him. Like, what if he got caught up in some cartel shit or was in an accident? It was so out of character for him to ignore her, so she was starting to admit to herself that she was becoming worried. She wanted to appease her mother and then go on about her day.

With one last look in the mirror, she grabbed her sunglasses and left her room in search of her mother.

A loud outburst from Mateo startled Blanca out of her sleep. She shot up in bed, sitting straight up as she looked around, trying to figure out what the fuck was going on. One glance at her phone told her it was nearing eleven in the morning. They had stayed up all damn night fucking and talking about the future, Blanca doing everything she could to down Lux and mind-fuck Mateo. It had been hard work, but she did that shit with pride and slept like a baby afterward.

Finally, she peered up at Mateo and saw that he was scowling angrily at her from across the room. In his hand was his cellphone that she had hidden in her purse. She smoothed her face into a mask void of emotion before she asked, "What's wrong?"

"Don't play fucking stupid, Blanca. What the fuck

is this?" he asked angrily as he lifted his phone into the air.

Blanca shrugged and then stretched her arms before answering. "Looks like your phone."

"Why the fuck was it turned off and in your purse?" Mateo seethed. He woke up that morning and realized he hadn't checked his phone in days. He was too drunk the first few days to notice, and too hungover yesterday to care, but that morning, he woke up with a clear head. When he couldn't find his phone, something in him kept nagging to check Blanca's purse. Sure enough, his phone was in there and turned completely off. His first thought was that maybe it just died, but when he was able to power it on and saw there were various calls and messages from Lux, his anger got the best of him.

Blanca slowly got out of bed and walked up to him, strutting like she was trying to be both sexy and look innocent. Mateo did nothing but glare at her. When she placed her hands on his chest, he stiffened and kept the mean mug on his face.

"Papi, I turned it off when you were on your drinking binge. No way did I want you to contact Lux and ruin everything in your state of mind. You might not remember your mood after Lux left for her job, but I do. I had to witness it firsthand," Blanca revealed as she stared up at him with wide eyes and a slight pout.

Mateo's features softened slightly before he looked down at his phone again. "There are messages here from her from that day, B. You said she hadn't called… why would you say that if she's been blowing me up this entire time? Shit is all fucked up… If I would have known she was trying to get ahold of me, I would have been squashed this shit."

Blanca clenched her jaw tightly. She wanted to snap at him, but she knew she couldn't. Besides, he needed to go back to Lux at some point, anyway… and soon. The wedding was coming up, and they technically weren't supposed to even be spending time together the past few days. The focus should have been on the wedding, but Blanca was selfish. She wanted it all. She sighed and said, "I turned your phone off as soon as you took your first shot. I knew it was going to be a shit show, and I was willing to let you feel that shit for a little while, so I put your phone in my purse so you wouldn't be tempted to do something you would regret. I honestly forgot about your phone, papi. Lux hasn't hit me up, so I kind of forgot about her, too. My main focus has been you."

Mateo's guard was down upon hearing her words, oblivious to the manipulation she was spitting at him. He sighed heavily and walked over to the bed before plopping down and burying his hands in his head. "How the fuck am I going to fix this shit? I really thought she didn't give a fuck about me... but seeing all these messages and shit makes me think otherwise. I'm fucking confused, man."

Blanca rolled her eyes since his head was down while he was rambling before masking her emotions and walking over to him. She kneeled in front of him and looked up into his eyes, waiting for him to give her his attention. When he finally did, she took his face in her hands and said, "Lux doesn't give a fuck about you, Mat. Let that be a known fucking fact. I am the only person left who loves you. All Lux cares about is her job and whatever guy she's fucking on, so what we are going to do is craft up a story... something you can tell her as to why you have been MIA the past few days. Once you are back on her good side, we are going to go through with the plan next week. You will marry Lux, and as soon as all the finances are settled, I will kill her. We will walk away with all her money and move some-where else... maybe the US, eh? Have a few babies, get a couple puppies... we will put all this bullshit behind us. There's nothing left here for you, anyway, Mat. Now that your parents are gone, all you have is me."

Mateo thought about what she said. He had half a

mind to fully believe what she was saying. It sounded good, and he honestly didn't even doubt it was true. Her plan could work, and he could eventually learn to be happy after he got over what he did to Lux, but another part of him, a much smaller part, was hesitant. Maybe if he could find proof that Lux was cheating on him, this would be easier. He decided to straight up ask Blanca. "Has Lux ever mentioned there being someone else?"

Without hesitating, Blanca lied. "Well... there was this one time..."

Mateo's brows furrowed. "What one time? Y'all are always talking that girl talk and shit. B, if you know something... tell me."

"It was right before your parents died, Mat. I wanted to tell you, but then they died, and I didn't think it was the best idea to crush you even more, but she did mention that... well..."

"Spit that shit out, B," Mateo snapped. He wasn't mad at her. He just wanted to know the truth once and for all.

"She slipped up and told me she wasn't a virgin like everyone thought. She said she had sex for the first time not too long ago, and she loved it. She wouldn't say with who, but she claimed they never saw each other again. For all I know, she was lying, though. All these so-called jobs just seem so suspicious…"

Mateo's head was reeling. All this time he was feeling guilty for fucking around with Blanca, and Lux was out here being just as grimy and giving it up to the next man. Maybe she wasn't plotting on his demise like he was with her, but at this point, Mateo refused to feel guilty about that. Blanca watched in pure happiness at the visible shift in Mateo. Her lie was working, and she couldn't be happier. Finally, Mateo said, "Damn."

"I know, papi, I wanted to tell you… it just didn't feel right," Blanca replied innocently.

Mateo looked down at her and caressed her face. "None of this is your fault, baby. Thank you for telling me, but what are we going to say to her? It's been going on four days since I last talked to her. This shit has to be good if we are going to follow through with this and end this shit once and for all."

Blanca nodded in agreement and gave a small victory smile. It was so easy getting Mateo right where she needed him to be. Her victory smile turned into a devilish one as she moved her hand to the waistband of his boxers, tugging on them. He lifted automatically, and she freed his dick that was already hardening.

"How about we come up with that after we cum?

You know I think better after being freshly fucked," Blanca replied.

Mateo smirked. Even though his heart was aching at the news he just got, Blanca always knew what to do and say to get him right. He laid back and put his arms behind his head. "Do ya thing, baby."

Blanca did just that. She sucked his dick until his toes curled before climbing on top of him and riding them both into an orgasmic oblivion. All that could be heard through the room were the sounds of their moans, while Blanca thought up a lie good enough to get Mateo back into Lux's good graces.

ux enjoyed breakfast with her mother, but she refused to allow Dionne to make it go on longer than it needed to. Lux didn't rush to eat, and she entertained her mother's conversation. She even took part in reminiscing about Lux's childhood and planning for the future, since Lux was due to move out after the wedding, as long as it still happened. But when Dionne tried insisting that they take a swim, Lux drew the line.

"Mama, I have some stuff to handle. We can take a swim another time. I promise," Lux said, standing from the blanket where they had been sitting for the last couple of hours. There was a picnic spread out over the blanket, and Lux looked down at the mess and asked, "Do you want some help cleaning up?"

Dionne peered up at her daughter and sighed before waving her off. "No, girl. Go do whatever you have to do. I hope the shit doesn't bite you in the ass."

Lux giggled. "Mama! It's going to be fine. I just want to find him so I can talk to him and figure out if I'm getting married next week or not. That's it. I'll come find you once we talk. I love you."

"Yeah, yeah," Dionne mumbled. "I love you, too. Send your father out here to help me out with this mess."

"Yes, ma'am," Lux replied before turning on her heels and making her way toward their house. Once she made it inside, she walked through the halls until she came up on the door for her father's man cave. She knew he would be in there because it was where he spent most of his time if he wasn't up under her mother. She knocked once and then waited for him to answer.

"Come in!" he yelled.

Lux pushed open the door and waved at her father, who was sitting on the leather couch that sat in front of a mounted TV screen. He was watching a rerun game of his favorite sport, baseball. He would watch old games all the time if there weren't new ones on to enjoy. He was obsessed, and Lux got a kick out of seeing him so into something so normal that didn't have to do with weapons or harming someone else.

"Hi, Papa," Lux greeted. "Mama wants your help cleaning up down at the beach."

Waylan's head fell back against the sofa as he groaned before peering at his daughter. "I suppose you're not helping because you're about to track Mateo down?"

Lux giggled. Her father knew her too well. "I think Mama is mad at me for doing it, but I just want to find him so we can talk. She acts like I'm trying to kill the man."

Waylan waved Lux off at the mention of Dionne. "Don't mind your mother. She doesn't understand us as well as she likes to think. If she had the skills we did, she would put them to use, too. Trust me."

Lux nodded in agreement. "Did you ever track Mama down and pop up on her?"

Waylan chuckled. "I tracked her down more times than I will ever admit, but I didn't pop up on her. I knew better than that. I just kept tabs on her to make sure she was okay and that she wasn't trying to run from me."

Lux chuckled. "I don't blame you. It's hard not to cross that line, but I've done good so far."

"You have, which is why I went ahead and tracked Mateo myself. I didn't want you to cross that line. Don't be like me, nena. Be better," Waylan replied.

Lux's smile was wide as she eyed her father from the doorway. "Papa, you didn't have to do that."

He shrugged. "I wanted to. Something about the way Mateo acted last time we saw him didn't sit right with me. I wanted to make sure he was really just cooling off and not doing some other shit."

"Other shit like what, old man?" Lux giggled. "You're more paranoid than me, I swear."

"I would rather be too paranoid than not aware," Waylan replied. "Remember to never put anything past anyone, mija. You know this. People are devious and evil, and the only person you are in charge of protecting is yourself. If you can protect your old man and mama, too, then fine."

They both chuckled at that. Lux walked over to her father and patted him on his back. "I'll always protect you, Papa."

He smiled up at her. "I did good with you, Lux. I am so proud of you."

Lux was taken aback by his kind words. That was out of the normal for him, but it seemed the older he got, especially since the last job he took that went wrong, he seemed to express his feelings more often, and it always warmed Lux's heart. "Thank you, Papa."

He nodded. "Mateo has been in a hotel for the

past few days. Did you know he had a room reserved for about a year now?"

Lux's brows furrowed. "No, that's odd."

Waylan shrugged. "Not really. You have to remember he lived with his parents until they died and then with us. He probably just wanted a place to get away where he could be alone."

Lux realized that made sense, so she didn't think much else about it. She was actually mad she never thought about doing that herself, but her parents' respected her privacy, so there really wasn't a need for it. "What hotel?"

"The one Blanca works at," he replied. "I'll text you the room number."

"Thanks again, Papa," Lux said, leaning down to kiss his cheek.

"Anything for you."

"You'd better go help Mama before she comes in here fussing," Lux said as she straightened up and headed for the door.

"How much help does she expect me to be with one good arm?" Waylan asked as he stood and gestured to his arm that was still sitting snuggly in a sling.

Lux giggled, but didn't respond, because she knew her father was going to go outside and help his wife as best he could. She didn't even bother going back to her room to change. She simply walked toward the front door. Once she was outside, she got into her car and started it up, pulling out of her driveway and toward Blanca's job. While she was thinking of Blanca, she dialed her number while she was on the way there to see if her friend was working, but she didn't answer. She wondered if she should pick up an early lunch for Blanca since it was a little after eleven now, but since she wasn't sure if she was even working, she continued with her initial mission.

It didn't take long for her to get to the hotel Blanca worked at. She parked and took a look at her phone. Her father stuck true to his word and sent her a text with the room number. Lux wasted no time grabbing her purse and phone and getting out of the car. It was hot as hell that day, and the sun was shining brightly as she walked into the hotel. She waved at Mary, who was working the front desk. She didn't see Blanca, so she didn't stop to chat. Instead, she kept moving toward the elevator.

The lobby of the hotel was beautifully decorated with cool blue colors with pops of yellow, much like her room. If she ever had a need to stay in a hotel in her hometown, she would have chosen this one as well. It was clean, high end, and decorated to her tastes. One thing about her future husband… he had good taste. His parents made sure of that.

Once she was in the elevator, she pressed the button for the top floor and waited patiently as it slowly made its way up the building. She was glad nobody else was on the elevator with her to slow the process of getting to Mateo. While she waited in the elevator, she dug around in her purse to see if she had a listening device. She normally carried one with her out of habit, much like she typically carried a gun and a few other things she might need on the job. She realized in her haste to leave the house she forgot her gun, but she did have a knife, a lock pick, and a listening device. She put the device in her ear and got off the elevator when the doors opened. She really just wanted to make sure Mateo wasn't meeting with someone from his family business or some shit before she knocked. His having this hotel room booked for almost a year now made her wonder if he sometimes did business here. She had no clue what he typically did in the way of work, and she never asked because she didn't want her same questions to be directed at her. Besides, she knew when they got married, they would talk all that shit out, and they might even start taking up more of a role in each other's businesses. Still, the last thing she wanted to do was pop up on Mateo and embarrass him if he was with an associate, so when she got to the door, she grabbed her phone out of her purse and paired the listening device to her phone so she could control the volume. She stood still and listened once she got the volume right, and right away, she heard voices.

"There are messages here from her from that day, B. You said she hadn't called… why would you say that if she's been blowing me up this entire time? Shit is all fucked up… If I would have known she was trying to get ahold of me, I would have been squashed this shit."

Lux's brows pulled together as she listened. *Who the fuck is Mateo talking about? I know the fuck like hell it's not me… and who is he talking to? It can't be…* Lux's thoughts were interrupted by another voice. A woman's voice.

"I turned your phone off as soon as you took your first shot. I knew it was going to be a shit show, and I was willing to let you feel that shit for a little while, so I put your phone in my purse so you wouldn't be tempted to do something you would regret. I honestly forgot about your phone, papi. Lux hasn't hit me up, so I kind of forgot about her, too. My main focus has been you."

Lux was confused. Why would Blanca's main concern be Mateo? And why didn't she tell Lux she had seen Mateo when they talked briefly the other day? Shit wasn't adding up, and Lux's heart was dropping with each word that was spoken. She forced herself to keep a clear head until she could get the full picture.

"How the fuck am I going to fix this shit? I really thought she didn't give a fuck about me... but seeing all these messages and shit makes me think otherwise. I'm fucking confused, man," Lux heard Mateo say through the listening device.

Hell, that makes two of us, papi, Lux thought as she continued to listen.

"Lux doesn't give a fuck about you, Mat. Let that be a known fucking fact. I am the only person left who loves you. All Lux cares about is her job and whatever guy she's fucking on, so what we are going to do is craft up a story... something you can tell her as to why you have been MIA the past few days. Once you are back on her good side, we are going to go through with the plan next week. You will marry Lux, and as soon as all the finances are settled, I will kill her. We will walk away with all her money and move somewhere else... maybe the US, eh? Have a few babies, get a couple puppies... we will put all this bullshit behind us. There's nothing left here for you, anyway, Mat. Now that your parents are gone, all you have is me."

And there it was. The bombshell that completely shattered Lux. She felt like she couldn't breathe as she listened to the two people she loved most in the world plot on her in the worst ways. She was confused as fuck, but underneath all that confusion and pain was anger. A dangerous anger that was simmering just below the surface.

Lux felt like she was listening under water or some shit as the two traitors continued their conversation about her, not even knowing they just made the most deadly enemy known to man. Their voices sounded muffled as she tried to focus so she could hear. The blood rushing through her caused her eardrums to beat, and it was fucking with her. She strained to listen as she tried to calm her nerves.

"Has Lux ever mentioned there being someone else?" Mateo asked. Lux scoffed at his question. He should know better. She thought he knew her better. Her heart was breaking. A normal bitch would have been a mess of tears on the floor by now, but not Lux. Lux Rose didn't cry… Lux Rose got even.

"Well… there was this one time…" Lux reared back. And what the fuck was Blanca on? The bitch was spewing lies left and right, and Lux spotted right away that she was filling Mateo's head with some bullshit. Probably had been for years, from the sound of it. She couldn't believe what she was hearing. Lux wasn't the type to not notice something like this… but she had. Love made her blind, and it almost caused her downfall.

"What one time? Y'all are always talking that girl talk and shit. B, if you know something… tell me."

"It was right before your parents died, Mat. I wanted to tell you, but then they died, and I didn't think it was the best idea to crush you even more, but she did mention that… well…"

Don't do it, bitch, Lux thought. She wanted to see how far her ex-best friend was willing to take this shit.

"Spit that shit out, B."

"She slipped up and told me she wasn't a virgin like everyone thought. She said she had sex for the first time not too long ago, and she loved it. She wouldn't say with who, but she claimed they never saw each other again. For all I know, she was lying, though. All these so-called jobs just seem so suspicious…"

Lux was a crazy bitch when she needed to be. She laughed out loud at the bullshit that just slipped from Blanca's mouth. She knew there could be no way Mateo would believe that. She didn't care what the relationship between Mateo and Blanca was. Mateo had to have known her better than that. But the next words spoken were the final jab to Lux's heart. It was the nail in the coffin to the life she previously knew.

"Damn," Mateo said.

"I know, papi, I wanted to tell you… it just didn't feel right."

"None of this is your fault, baby. Thank you for telling me, but what are we going to say to her? It's been going on four days since I last talked to her. This shit has to be good if we are going to follow through with this and end this shit once and for all."

Lux shook her head in disbelief as she continued to listen while trying to process what the fuck was going on.

"How about we come up with that after we cum? You know I think better after being freshly fucked," Blanca replied, and Lux almost threw up the entire breakfast she had eaten with her mother. Not needing to hear shit else, she quickly snatched the device from her ear before stuffing it back into her purse. She stood there for a moment, wondering what her next move should be. She knew what the fuck she wanted to do. In fact, she looked down into her purse and palmed the knife and lock pick, but she shook her head. She knew better. The only time to commit a murder was when there was a one hundred percent chance she would get away from it. She couldn't do shit right now. Not here. There were too many witnesses, which only pissed her off further.

Instead of acting on her deadly instinct, she stuffed that away for now before backtracking down the hall and calling for the elevator. Once she was back in the lobby, she rushed through it and got into her car, slamming the door and gripping the steering wheel. Her mind raced as she thought about her best friend and soon to be husband. She felt like a fucking fool, and one thing niggas were about to learn… making Lux Rose out to be a fool would be the last mothafuckin' thing they ever did.

To be Continued…

 AUTHOR NOTE

I already know you are more than ready for the final installment! Don't worry, it's coming SOON! I can't wait to show you all what Lux has in store. Thank you for rocking with me through this mini-series! Y'all are so DOPE!

Stay tuned!
 Cyn

Up Next...

CYN'S CATALOG

Get signed copies at: Cynful Monarch

Dust 2 Diamonds

The Baddest of Them All

Lil Red Ryder

Rebel & Her Beast

A Fairytale Wedding

The Princess & the Goon

The Urban Fairytale Series Complete Collection

Baby, it's Cold Outside

Bosses Link Up

Billion Dollar Baddie

Billion Dollar Baddie 2

A Hood Chick's Savior

Anything for the Family

Anything for the Family 2

Endlessly Mine

Hell Hath No Fury: Beaten at Your Own Game

The Married Woman

Lux Rose: Born to Kill

LET'S CONNECT!

Join my readers group on Facebook, and stay up on
all releases, get character visuals and sneak peeks,
and even get in on giveaways!
https://www.facebook.com/
groups/277463019954112/

Sign up for my email list! Get exclusive content and
discounts!
https://bit.ly/39tvXOC

WHILE YOU'RE WAITING...

IF YOU LIKE FEMALE ASSASSINS...

Bosses Link Up: The Deadly Divas
The first 2 chapters

Nova

I hated driving at night. The way the streetlights reflected off everything and glared right into my vision truly had me fucked up and don't get me started on the rain. The shit was just further pissing me off. I couldn't wait to handle this lil' bit of business and get on with my night. I was hungry as hell and ready to curl up in bed with my dog, Marshmallow.

Luckily, I was almost at the location where the job was set up and it would only take a few minutes. I squinted my eyes as I crept down the crowded street, looking for the lounge I was meeting my client at. It was a Friday night and Queens was poppin'. Low key, I wished I could join all the fine ass men and pretty bitches that roamed the streets, but rule number one of the business I was in was to never stay on location for longer than necessary.

I spotted the lounge that my client owned on the corner. I pulled around the back and into the alley where I was instructed to park. There were a few other cars back there, so I angled the vehicle I was riding around in, to make for an easy getaway. Before getting out of the hooptie, I checked myself out in the mirror. My face automatically scrunched up at the sight of my mud-brown eyes. I hated wearing these colored contacts because they hid my beautiful blue eyes, but blue eyes against my caramel-colored skin were too memorable. My auburn curls were notice-able as well, which was why I had a black wig on. I looked ordinary as fuck. The point was to blend in and to not look like my normal, badass self. I sighed and got out of the car. I hurried to the door, so I didn't get too wet from the rain, as I silently hoped this shit didn't take more than twenty minutes. Not that I had much to go home to, but still.

I was a loner by choice. My dog was my best friend, and I really didn't feel like I needed anyone else. I enjoyed my own company, and I wasn't keen on the idea to answer to anyone else or do things on other people's time, which was why my love life was nonexistent. I didn't have time for a man to be all up under me with the job I had. In my opinion, all men were good for was dick. End of story.

I turned the rusted handle on the door and just like my client said, it was unlocked. I pushed it open and heard the music thumping in the lounge. I couldn't help but to move to the beat as my six-inch heels clicked against the tiled floor. I loved music. My body automatically swayed to the beat any and every time a melody would play. I bopped my head up and down and fought the urge to snap my fingers as I moved down a short hall toward a staircase that I knew would lead to the offices upstairs.

As I moved up the stairs I pulled a small handgun with a silencer attached to the barrel from my Hermes purse that was slung over my shoulder. I hated carrying this big ass bag with me, but my tight jeans and purple crop-top didn't leave much room for the tools I needed to complete my jobs. Compromising my fashion just wasn't going to happen. I was a boss ass bitch and I would dress the part no matter where I was or what I was doing.

I slowed down and stopped vibing to the music the second my stiletto hit the landing to the upper part of the building. It was time to focus. I trained my ears so I could hear any noises coming from the office straight ahead. I couldn't hear anything over the muffled music that played from downstairs, so I proceeded with caution.

The plan was simple. My client, Surge, was going to be in his office, which was directly in front of me, with his homeboy, Gio. In my business I quickly realized how grimy people really were, which was why I didn't trust anyone and the *exact* reason I stuck to myself. See, my job was to walk up in that office and kill Gio. Once the job was completed, Surge would give me fifteen thousand dollars, which was just the last half of his payment. Surge wasn't shit in my eyes, but that didn't matter at all to me. The only thing I was worried about was him paying me. I would never understand how people could set their friends and family up to die, but these dirty mothafuckas were the reason I was only twenty-four years old and rolling in dough. I really couldn't complain.

I crept toward the office and aimed my gun in front of me before forcefully pushing the door open. It took me a moment to comprehend the scene before me, and when I did I instantly got pissed. Both Surge and Gio were in the room, as planned. The only issue was that there was someone else in the room and Surge had a bullet in his head. His dead eyes stared straight through me. I felt my face morph into a mask of pure rage.

There was a bitch standing beside where Surge's body was slumped over in his office chair behind his desk. She had a gun in her hand and a smirk on her face while she talked to Gio as if there weren't a dead body in the room.

"What the fuck," I retorted and aimed my gun straight at the bitch.

"Shit," Gio cursed when he saw me.

He knew what the fuck was up. The chick just stared at me with a stony gaze. I peeped game right away. She had on a red wig, and I was guessing her eyes weren't actually blue. Judging by the clean shot straight through Surge's tempo and the way she was carelessly carrying on a conversation with Gio only moments ago told me everything I needed to know. This bitch was a hit woman. I'd never run across another bitch that did what I did in New York, especially not a one just as pretty as me. Even with her disguise, I could tell she was a bad bitch, which made me hate her more. Instantly. There was a reason I was consistent with the hires and highly recommended on the streets. It was because my marks never saw me coming. I had the face of an angel, even when I muted my looks. I naturally looked like I couldn't hurt a fly. It made me ten times more deadly and this chick in front of me seemed to have that shit down pat herself. I always gave props to a bad bitch when I saw one, but not when she was fucking with my money.

Speaking of money, there was only one thing on my mind. Who the fuck was going to pay me the other fifteen thousand dollars owed to me? Best believe I was about to kill Gio and this bitch, too, but with Surge dead there was no way for me to get my money.

Maybe I can keep Gio alive and make him pay me for sparing his life, I thought, but I was interrupted when

Gio caught me off-guard and charged toward me. I swung my gun on him and fired a shot. Gio yelped in pain at the same time the chick on the other side of the room raised her gun and aimed it at me.

"Don't move," she said calmly, as if she had everything under control.

Okay, now I was livid. Who the fuck did this bitch think she was? More than anything I wanted to turn my gun toward her and shoot her between the eyes, but instead, I kept my gun trained on Gio. I chanced a glance over at him and noticed that I had only shot him in the leg. *Shit.*

"Who the fuck are you?" I asked through gritted teeth as I averted my gaze back at the woman. She was wearing black skinny jeans with chunky knee-high-heeled boots. Her black t-shirt was snug over her chest, showcasing her ample breasts. I had to admit that her style was on point.

"Bitch, the question is who the fuck are you?" she asked with her head cocked to the side.

"I dare you to call me a bitch again," I said through gritted teeth.

"Bi—" she said, but a gunshot interrupted her.

I ducked, realizing Gio had been the one to shoot. He narrowly missed me, and I knew one thing was for sure... this shit was not worth losing my life over. I half crawled, half ran toward the door and yanked it open as soon as my fingertips grazed it. I stood up fully and sprinted down the stairs.

My senses were on high alert because my ears quickly picked up on the fact that someone was running after me. I glanced behind me and realized it was the hoe from upstairs. I had half of a mind to shoot the bitch before she could make it all the way down the stairs. It was dark as hell in the hallway. I had issues driving at night and best believe that a bitch could shoot a gun and hit her target every single time in *any* conditions, but I heard sirens approaching. It was then that I realized the music from the lounge had been cut, and there was pandemonium happening within the main part of the club.

Gio's dumb ass didn't have a silencer like me and the other chick did, so his gunshot alerted not only the people in the establishment, but the police as well. I decided to get the fuck out of dodge. I could worry about Gio and his bitch another time. I pushed the back door open and made it inside the car I came in within a few seconds. I cranked the engine and peeled out of the alley, noticing that the woman was right behind me in another car. I turned right, and she turned left.

Twenty minutes later I pulled into a junkyard where my actual car was sitting, looking pretty as hell with its sparkling gold paint and chrome rims. I hopped out of the hooptie and tossed the keys onto the seat before closing the door and climbing into my own car.

My night had been completely ruined, but it wouldn't be the last time I saw those two. I would track Gio down, get my money, and finish the job for the simple fact that the asshole had shot at me. Nobody who had the balls to fire a gun at me *ever* lived to speak about it.

Another thirty minutes later, I pulled into the driveway of my home and made a mental note to ask around and figure out who the new bitch was. I was extremely territorial and if she was getting jobs that could have been coming my way and putting money in my pockets then I needed to dead that problem. Literally and immediately.

ZURI

Fuck, I thought after hooking a sharp right onto a narrow side street. Two bitches in the same city killing for cash seemed unreal. I could assume the chick from the lounge was in the same business as me because I was getting major boss bitch vibes from her. A part of me wanted to blast her brains on sight, but the business side of me opposed. Giving away a free blow to the head was comparable to trashing thirty grand. Every dollar counted and so did every fucking bullet. Besides, her tardiness only helped me. I would meet up with Gio in the morning to collect my payment, and that would already feel like a win. The other bitch wouldn't be able to get the rest of her money, if she even got a dollar to begin with.

Pulling into an alleyway, I parked the fucked up Camry that I paid a crackhead to use next to the dumpster. I turned the key to deescalate the engine and left the key sitting in the ignition. As I opened the squeaking door, the sound of a vehicle entering the alleyway was brought to my attention. The bright headlights made it impossible for me to get a clear view through the rearview mirror. I snatched the gun from my lap and got out of the car. My left boot was met with the pavement and the other boot joined before I pointed my weapon toward my visitor and aimed it at the center of their windshield. I angled my body toward them as I kept a tight hug on the trigger and was ready to shoot, but once the person got closer, I recognized who it was and lowered the gun to my thigh. It was only Taz.

"Yo, you were really gonna shoot me?" Taz spat once I was in the Escalade's backseat.

"I have to keep my eyes open at all times," I explained as I snatched the itchy red wig from my head.

"I guess, but it ain't like you didn't know I was coming."

"Why didn't you tell me there was another bitch in this neck of the woods doing the same thing as me?" I questioned, ignoring his statement as I removed the black leather gloves from my manicured hands.

"You wouldn't have given a fuck! This has been your career ever since you were in Atlanta. A move to New York excited you. More drugs and more crime means more money for you."

He was right. Receiving the news that my

husband would have to relocate didn't seem like a bad idea all around. He was promoted, and they almost tripled his annual salary. Signing the deal with the company increased his pay the second he laid ink onto the contract. Besides the high increase in pay, we received a moving bonus in the form of a check worth ten-thousand dollars. Aside from the money, it allowed a reunion between us and Zeek's brother, Taz. In Atlanta, Taz and I worked together. It pissed me off when he made his move back to their hometown in New York. Doing shit alone meant more work for me, which was the opposite of what I stood for. I liked easy, dirty ass money.

"Well, a heads up would have been nice," I replied. "The bitch was there, and she almost took Gio out. I have no doubt had she succeeded, then I would have been next. That was a botched job if I ever saw one."

"My bad," Taz said nonchalantly, and I shook my head.

I rested my knees onto the seat and leaned over the backrest to grab my raven tinted Adidas duffle bag from the trunk behind me. I latched onto the strap and pulled the bag toward my chest before throwing it next to me on the seat. I pulled out my all black long sleeve nylon bodysuit after I plopped my ass back down. I brought my knees to my chest so I could unzip my boots. Once they were off, I slid my jeans down my thighs and pulled my t-shirt over my head, leaving me in only my Nike ankle socks and Victoria's Secret undergarment set.

"What do you think my brother would do if he found out I've seen you naked?" Taz joked as he moved his eyes back and forth between the road and his rearview mirror.

"Shit! I'd charge a mothafucka to look at this badass body. You better be glad you get to see it for free! Even your brother spends bags on my ass!" I exclaimed in a cocky manner as I inched the bodysuit past my torso.

I glared out through the tinted window and noticed we were entering Yonkers. I quickly slid my toes into the burgundy, fur-coated UGG boots that were lifted from the bottom of the bag. I gathered the outfit I discarded onto the floor in the back and scrambled to load the items into the duffle bag. Once the bag was secured by the zipper, I threw it over the headrest of the seat causing a thumping echo to express throughout the vehicle.

I always changed my clothes. Not only did it make the task force's job harder to catch me, but it also allowed Zeek to remain blindsided to my actual job title. Telling my husband about my line of work would have me fucked up. Although he and Taz grew up around gangs and drug lords, he'd always been far from street smart. I made a vow to myself to *never* allow him to find out about his killer wife. He could continue thinking I was a stripper. I'd rather deal with his snarled remarks as opposed to dealing with an interrogation from him any day.

Sometimes I wondered why I married him to begin with, but then I remembered the amount of cash he always flaunted. I would say it was his charm and good looks, but he looked almost identical to Taz. Dark skin tone, muscular build, and sleek hair waves. Honestly, if I would have met his brother before him, then I would've snatched his ass up first. He was the type of man I would normally go for. Street smart and sexy as fuck. Another good thing about being married to Zeek was the fact that his large pockets were a good coverup for my money trail. If I were to ever be questioned, then his direct deposits could count for the thousands I spent on Armani, Gucci, and Louis Vuitton.

Taz made a right onto a quiet, dark street which informed me we were almost at my house. Lifting the gun from the seat, I detached the silencer and stuffed the gun into one of my UGG boots. I slid the silencer onto the other. Within two minutes we were approaching the gate to my mansion. After Taz put the code into the code box we waited as the gates slid open. Once it was clear to drive, Taz cruised down the driveway leaving the gates to close behind the vehicle.

"Rememb—," I attempted to say after the car came to a stop, but was interrupted.

"I know already. Have your clothes cleaned. How long we been doing this shit together again?"

"Bye, Taz! Be here around eleven so we can meet Gio for the rest of my money," I ordered.

Before tugging on the door handle, I lifted my Coach purse from the floorboard. I slammed the rear door shut after I got out of the vehicle. Throwing the strap to my purse over my shoulder, I strutted toward the front door of my house. I entered the code into the box on the door before I heard the lock unlatch from its panel. I twisted the knob and entered the foyer of my mansion. I closed the door behind me and walked straight up the stairs before taking a right turn. I tiptoed down the hallway with my head held high while tightening my abdomen muscles. Remaining quiet was more than necessary. Slowly, I turned the knob on the office door and entered. I left the door cracked as I rushed to my safe.

I unlocked it and pulled my gun and its silencer from my boots before resting them on the top shelf.

A shower was much needed. Once the safe was locked back up, I left the office and strode toward the opposite end of the hallway to approach the master bedroom. I noticed my husband wasn't in bed after I opened the door and walked inside. A streak of light shone from underneath the bathroom door, and I was able to confirm his presence.

"Babe! I'm home," I yelled to inform him so he didn't think I was some type of intruder or some shit.

"Hey, baby. You make a lot of money tonight?" Zeek asked after he opened the door and stood in the entryway in nothing but a pair of boxers.

"Hell yeah," I smirked as I propped the Coach bag on top of my makeup vanity.

"I still don't understand why you want to be a fucking stripper. If I'm straight, you're straight."

I knew it was coming. I rolled my eyes and then turned to face Zeek, who walked across the room to join me. Directing my eyes toward his dick, the nine inches of pleasure stood at attention. With the tip of my inch-long nail on my index finger, I shifted the hole of his plaid boxers to the side, exposing his manhood. I licked my lips as I admired his package. One thing I could never say was that he wasn't blessed. I removed my finger from his boxers. Seductively, I trailed my eyes along his abdomen muscles until I connected with his glossy, midnight eyes. Instead of feeding off of my vibe, he tilted his head and brought his eyebrows toward the bridge of his nose.

"What?" I asked after snapping my neck back.

He used his thumb to wipe my cheek.

"Is that blood?" he questioned after he brought his finger to my face.

Immediately, I turned to face the mirror on my vanity. Sure enough, it was fucking blood. I was definitely going to put the blame on that bitch for showing up. She put a wrench in my natural flow of things and all over again anger unleashed from my soul.

I gotta catch this bitch and end her career, I thought. The sloppiness of what went down showed, and I couldn't allow it to happen again.

"Yes," I blandly answered Zeek's question.

"What the fuck happened?"

"There was a fight at the club tonight. I guess I was too close," I lied, making up a scene off the top of my head.

"Gotta be careful, baby," Zeek advised before curling my chin into his palm and kissing my soft pink lips.

Careful? Oh, I was going to be careful alright.

Carefully take my fucking pistol and place it to the bitch's dome! Costing my peace came with a price. A thirty-thousand dollar fucking bullet resting in her skull, to be exact. I say it's an expensive ass souvenir to take to a grave.

Hey There!

Thank you for your support on my literary journey. I hope your reading experience was a pleasant one. Please leave a review on Goodreads and Amazon. Please feel free to connect with me to stay current on upcoming releases and reader specific exclusives.